S0-BOC-401

GEORGE
the Drummer Boy

An I Can Read Book®

GEORGE
the Drummer Boy
by Nathaniel Benchley
Pictures by Don Bolognese

HarperCollins*Publishers*

HarperCollins®, ☕®, and I Can Read Book®
are trademarks of HarperCollins Publishers Inc.

GEORGE THE DRUMMER BOY
Text copyright © 1977 by Nathaniel Benchley
Illustrations copyright © 1977 by Don Bolognese

All rights reserved. No part of this book may be used or reproduced in any manner whatsoever without written permission except in the case of brief quotations embodied in critical articles and reviews. Printed in the United States of America. For information address HarperCollins Children's Books, a division of HarperCollins Publishers, 10 East 53rd Street, New York, NY 10022.

Library of Congress Cataloging-in-Publication Data
Benchley, Nathaniel, date
  George the drummer boy.

  (An I can read history book)
  SUMMARY: A view of the incidents at Lexington and Concord, Massachusetts, which were the start of the American Revolution, as seen from the eyes of George, a British drummer boy.
  1. Lexington, Battle of, 1775—Juvenile fiction. 2. Concord, Battle of, 1775—Juvenile fiction. [1. Lexington, Battle of, 1775—Fiction. 2. Concord, Battle of, 1775—Fiction. 3. United States—History—Revolution, 1775-1783—Campaigns and battles—Fiction] I. Bolognese, Don. II. Title.
PZ7.B4312Ge   [E]   76-18398
ISBN 0-06-020500-8
ISBN 0-06-020501-6 (lib. bdg.)

GEORGE
the Drummer Boy

George was a drummer boy

with the King's soldiers.

They were stationed in Boston.

Two hundred years ago,

Boston belonged to England.

7

The Boston people

did not like the taxes

the King made them pay.

Since they could not show their anger

to the King,

they showed it to his soldiers.

George wanted to be friends

with the people.

But it was hard to be friends.

All they did was shout

and throw things

at the soldiers.

9

A spy told the British commander,

"People are hiding cannon

and gunpowder in Concord."

Concord was a town

about twenty miles from Boston.

The commander, General Gage,

decided to send troops out

to capture all the cannon and powder

they could find.

He made his plans in secret,

so the people

would be taken by surprise.

First,

he picked two companies of soldiers,

and said they were going to have

special training.

George's company was one of these.

When he heard the news,

he went to see his friend Fred.

"What does it mean?" he asked.

"No idea," Fred replied.

"Why not ask someone?" said George.

"In the Army you don't ask questions,"
Fred said.

"You do as they tell you."

Next, General Gage had men fix
the barges and long boats.
"Maybe this means we go to sea,"
George said.
"I hope not," said Fred.
"Unless, of course,
they take us home."

Three nights later,

after the soldiers had gone to bed,

they were wakened,

and told to get dressed.

16

"What kind of training is this?"
George asked.

"Do they want us to play owls?"

"Don't ask," said Fred.

"Just dress."

The moon was bright.

They could see the barges

that would take them

across the water.

George had his drum,

but since they were told to be quiet,

he didn't use it.

He just waited

to see what would happen next.

They crowded
into the boats and barges,
and were rowed
across the Charles River
to Charlestown.

It was early spring,

and the wind from the east was cold.

George sat close to Fred,

to keep warm.

In Charlestown, they waded ashore
through water up to their knees,
and then they waited.
They waited for two hours,
standing around shivering
in the cold.

Behind them, in Boston,

George saw two lights in the spire

of the Old North Church.

"I wonder what they mean," he said.

"Most likely they're a signal,"

said Fred.

"What for?" asked George.

"The General hasn't told me,"

Fred said.

George was too cold to laugh.

At last, they started to march.

Major Pitcairn was in charge

of George's company.

He told them

they were going to Concord,

to look for hidden guns and powder.

George sneezed.

"Shh," said Fred.

"You'll wake the countryside."

After a while, they could hear

the boom of cannon in the distance.

Far-off church bells were ringing.

Dim shapes of running men

went by them in the dark.

They heard

the thud of horses' hooves.

28

"I think they know we're coming,"
George said.

"I told you not to sneeze so loud,"
said Fred.

"Big joke," said George.

"I'm scared."

"Those lights we saw," said George.

"They must have been a signal
we were on our way."

"That's right," Fred replied.

"This may turn out
to be a long day."

Slowly, day began to break.

Birds chirped and twittered

in the trees.

When it was light enough,

George could see

blossoms on the apple trees

beside the road.

He could also see

the town of Lexington,

and men hurrying toward it

across the fields.

There were eighty Minutemen

on the Green.

They were called Minutemen

because they had to be ready

at a minute's notice.

They had guns.

All George had was his drum.

He hoped

there would not be a fight.

When the Minutemen saw

how many soldiers there were,

they started to move away.

Major Pitcairn

told his soldiers not to fire.

He shouted at the people

to disperse,

then moved his men in closer.

Someone, somewhere, fired a shot.

Nobody was hit,

but it started

the soldiers shooting.

They fired three volleys,

then broke ranks

and ran at the Minutemen.

Major Pitcairn

got his men back in order.

He marched them off toward Concord.

Eight Minutemen had been killed.

It had happened so fast

that George had no time

to be afraid.

In Concord

there were more Minutemen,

waiting on a hill

across a bridge.

There were more than at Lexington,

and still more were coming

every minute.

George began to wonder

what he was doing there.

"I wish I was back in Boston,"

he told Fred.

"Me, too," said Fred.

"I don't like this place
one little bit."

All the guns and powder
had been taken out of Concord,
and hidden someplace else.

George saw some soldiers

setting a fire.

"What are they doing that for?"

he asked.

"They have to do something,"

Fred replied.

"They can't come all this way

for nothing."

"It seems pretty silly to me,"

said George.

The Minutemen saw the smoke,

and thought

the town was being burned.

They charged down the hill

at the soldiers,

and the soldiers turned and fled.

"I knew that was a bad idea,"

George said, as he ran.

"Look what they started."

By now the Minutemen

were all around.

They fired

from behind fences and stone walls,

and picked the soldiers off

as they ran.

It seemed to George

that everywhere he looked

a Minuteman

was pointing a gun at him.

Fred shouted,

and dropped his gun.

A bullet had hit him in the arm.

"Are you all right?" George asked.

"Ask me later," Fred replied.

"This is no time for talk."

George picked up the gun,

and kept on running.

At Lexington,

they met more British soldiers,

who had come out from Boston

to help.

These soldiers had two cannons,
which kept the Minutemen away
until the others could escape.

It was dark and raining

by the time

they got back to Charlestown.

Nobody knew or cared

that this was the start

of the Revolution.

When it was over,

America would be

a country of its own.

All George and the others wanted

was to get back safely to Boston.

It had been,

as Fred said it might be,

a long day.

NOTE:

Just as it takes two sides to make a war, so there must be two stories for every battle. Sometimes they are alike. Other times they are wildly different. This is a guess at how the British soldiers felt before and during the battles at Lexington and Concord. As guesses go, it should not be too far wrong.

—N.B.